BUT,
WHEN IS CHRISTMAS COMING?

written by
HELEN SCOTT

illustrated by
DARRELL PULLIAM

published by
E³-MAGE PUBLISHING CO.

BUT,
WHEN IS CHRISTMAS COMING?

This edition first published in U.S. in 1997
by E³-Mage Publishing Co.
P. O. Box 2163, Country Club Hills IL 60478

ISBN: 0-9660051-0-4

Printed and bound in U.S.A.

For information about permission
about any of the material
in this book please contact:
Permissions Department
E³-Mage Publishing Co.
P. O. Box 2163
Country Club Hills, IL 60478

Author: Helen Scott
Illustrator: Darrell Pulliam
Designer: Dawn HoFung
Editor: Phyllis R. Horton

A NOTE FROM THE AUTHOR

Thank you for purchasing this delightful, colorful book. The story is real and was provided to me by both my 5- and 7-year-old daughters. To make this book more enjoyable for your audience, may I suggest reading it to children ages 5 and up. The realism of a child's determination and focus will enable even adults to appreciate and find the book pleasurable. For teachers and administrators, the book chronicles the major holidays celebrated in the United States. Not only are the holidays chronicled by calendar, but also the events synonymous with the particular holiday, with its meaning or reason, are briefly stated. The book can be used to teach the 'when and why' of holidays, using a fun form of medium. The book should be read with enthusiasm and excitement for a real appreciation for each experience to be shared between the main character, Bebi*, and you, the audience.

*The 'e' in Bebi is pronounced as the short 'e' in ever and the 'i' is pronounced as the long 'e' in even.

To Ebe, Elexus, Ebebi and all the children
whose books are not yet written:
We didn't know the WAY before now.

H.S.

BUT,
WHEN IS CHRISTMAS COMING?

Of all the holidays throughout the year, little Bebi DeLoach likes the Christmas holiday the most. Because, you see, on Christmas Day there is so much excitement and fun and toys and goodies to be shared by everyone! Bebi can always count on getting every toy she asks for on her Christmas list. She knows that on Christmas Day Mom makes all of her favorite foods and desserts, and if she wants to, she can taste them all day long. Auntie Kathy, Uncle Gus and cousin Kara visit and stay the whole day! Bebi can even count on her sisters and brother being extra nice to her. They don't tease her or bully her at all on this day. Why, it seems the whole world is nice on Christmas Day!

And so, during every other holiday, from the beginning of the year until the end of the year, Bebi waits and watches and looks for Christmas Day...

January 1 is called New Year's Day and is the first holiday of the year. But, on the day before New Year's Day, New Year's Eve, a huge celebration with parties is held by people everywhere. This celebration is to help bring the New Year in with a bang! At midnight, when the clock strikes 12:00, a new year begins. People do all kinds of wonderful, fun things to celebrate. They have parties, or go to the movies or cook special foods for their families. Some people watch great fireworks displays, where they see flares make the night sky light up bright! For the DeLoach family celebration, there are balloons to be blown up, noise makers to be bought and all kinds of good foods to be made by the women in the family. When all the relatives and friends begin to arrive for the party on this night, there is so much excitement! Everybody is ready for a good time—everybody except Bebi.

Bebi stands in the family room, sadly watching all the activities around her. Her sisters are helping Mom. Even her puppy, Kersh, seems happy that a new year is coming. All little Bebi can think of is that Christmas is over. She walks over to Mom, gently pulls on her skirt and asks in her little, squeaky voice, "But, when is **Christmas** coming again?" Mommy says, "Bebi, Christmas was just over. Christmas will be here again before you know it."

On January 15, Dr. Martin Luther King, Jr.'s birthday is being celebrated. There is no school on this day. Children don't have to wear their uniforms or wake up early. All schools and all government offices are closed because Dr. Martin Luther King, Jr. was so special that his birthday was made into a holiday. The children are happy to be out of school. They can visit the museums or go to different community centers to learn more about Dr. King and the work he did to make the world a better place. Mom and Dad stay home too. This is a day to remember all the wonderful things Dr. King did. Everybody is happy for a holiday and a day off from the week's routine—everybody except Bebi.

She looks at the pictures of Dr. King, looks around the house at her sisters and sadly says to Ebe, her big sister, "But, when is **Christmas** coming back?" Ebe tells her, "Christmas is coming Bebi. You just have to wait."

On February 14 everybody is excited about Valentine's Day! People give each other cards and candy or flowers and gifts to show their love on this day. The children are excited because they are going to have a party at school! They don't have to wear their uniforms either. Almost everybody wears something with hearts on it! There are red hearts on the girls' white, lacy socks. Some girls wear wide, cotton skirts with red and white hearts all over them. Even the bows on their skirts have little hearts on them. Some of the boys have hearts on their shirt pockets. At the party, the children make cards to give to their friends! They pass out candy hearts that say: "Be Mine." The teacher gives them red, strawberry-flavored lollipops shaped like hearts. All the children are excited to show how pretty and bright their cards are—except Bebi.

Bebi doesn't wear a dress or a skirt with hearts on it. She doesn't make any Valentine's Day cards. She draws a picture of Santa instead. When she hands her Santa picture to her best friend, Jazzy, she asks her, "But, when is **Christmas** coming?" Jazzy takes Bebi's hand and says, "I think Christmas will be next."

On March 17 everybody is excited about celebrating the Irish hero, Saint Patrick! People wear green and do all kinds of fun things with the color green to help celebrate. The big city pours green coloring into the river to make it turn all green! Some people even color their hair green! When Bebi goes to the grocery store with her Mom, she can smell delicious cookies. They are green and shaped like clover leaves! In the bakery section of the store, there are all kinds of yummy-looking cakes decorated with green toppings! All the store clerks have on green hats that look like the kind those little people called leprechauns wear. Everybody is having a fun time—everybody except Bebi.

Bebi likes cookies, but she doesn't want any green, clover-shaped cookies. Most of the time Bebi likes cake too. But, when Mom asks her if she wants a green cake to take home she says, "No." Bebi just wants to know about Christmas. When it's time to leave the store, she stands on her tiptoes and asks the store clerk, "But, do you know when is **Christmas** coming?" The clerk chuckles and smiles at her then says, "Honey, I'm sure Christmas is coming soon. It'll be here before you know it."

Easter Sunday, in early April, is the next holiday. Everybody is glad when Easter comes. The beginning of Spring is near, and soon you can go outside every day to play! On this holiday you can dress up in your very best dress, if you want to. The Park District has an Easter Egg hunt! The children wake up early so they won't miss any of the fun! Bebi's sister, Zindzi, is so excited, she wakes up first! She wants to fill her yellow straw basket, stuffed with pink play grass, with all the eggs she plans to find at the hunt. She gets the basket from the Easter Bunny. After the egg hunt, the Easter Bunny is there to take pictures with the children! Jelly Bean Clown, whose pockets are always filled with real fruit jelly beans, lets them look in his pockets for jelly beans and other treats to put in the baskets! Later, when they go home, they color more eggs and put on their Easter bonnets. Everybody is happy and so excited—everybody except Bebi.

She doesn't want to color any eggs. She doesn't want any jelly beans or other treats. When she sits to take a picture with the Easter Bunny, she looks at his milk chocolate face, his long, white, floppy ears and his big furry

feet. Then she puts her arm around his shoulder to get closer, and she whispers to Bunny, "Do you know when is **Christmas** coming?"

Easter Bunny smiles at her, then whispers back, "I'm sure Christmas is coming soon."

11

The next holiday, Memorial Day, is a really BIG holiday! All the flags are hung out in the towns to show that everybody cares about the people who served their country by doing things like flying airplanes, making machines and clothes and building bridges. Some people take flowers to cemeteries and put them on the graves of the ones they love. Preparations are being made for family picnics. Dad makes the first barbecue of the year! Mom, Dad and all the children look forward to being together for lots of outdoor fun! The children are even allowed to get out of school early so they can help get ready for the celebration. Everybody is excited —except Bebi.

She doesn't understand why her sisters ask what they should wear to the picnic. She doesn't feel like helping Mom pick a nice, red, juicy watermelon.

She can only ask Dad, "But when is **Christmas** coming?" Her dad says, "Christmas is a long way away Bebi. Let's try to have fun at the picnic now. But Christmas IS coming, honey."

Independence Day, on July 4, is the next holiday. This day is an important one in the United States because it is the country's birthday! To help celebrate, Dads and Uncles buy sparklers and firecrackers from Mr. Johnson's store. They light the fireworks when it gets dark outside. All the children have to sit far enough away from the fireworks so that they won't get hurt. Later, there is a really big fireworks display at the Community Park, with colorful flares that make loud noises and shower tiny bits of fire in the sky. The park supervisor lights these fireworks. Everybody wants to be sure to have a good seat to see the fireworks light up the night sky! Everybody picks something to wear that has the same colors as the American flag—red, white and blue. Dad and Bebi's brother, Cortez, have stripes on their shirts. Mom and Bebi's sisters have stars on their clothes. Everybody wants to join in the fun —everybody except Bebi.

Bebi is sad. All she can think about on any holiday is, "But, when is it going to be **Christmas** again?" Cortez, who knows why she is sad on holidays, puts his arm around her and says, "Christmas is coming soon Bebi. You'll see."

During the last week in August, it is time to go back to school. One week after school starts, on September 1, it's time to take a day off for Labor Day. On this day, working people can stay home so they can know how important their jobs are. All the things that bus drivers, lawyers, secretaries, teachers, business owners, bankers, doctors and other workers do is being celebrated. Hardly anybody has to work.

The big city is having a huge parade with all kinds of colorfully-decorated floats to show how much it cares about workers. The high school band marches in the parade and the band members play instruments! Everybody wants to go see the parade and to catch some candy that is thrown from the floats as they pass. The parade goes all the way to the park, where there are tall clowns on stilts, a magic show, balloons, cotton candy and all kinds of picnic food to eat! Everybody plans to have lots of fun!—except Bebi.

All little Bebi can think of is the fun she has on Christmas day. Sitting on the stairs of her house, she can hear the noises from the parade and the band playing. Still feeling sad, she asks Zindzi, "But, when is it going to be **Christmas**?" Zindzi takes a deep breath, then sighs and says to her, "Bebi, everybody keeps telling you—Christmas is coming, Christmas is coming. You just have to wait 'cause it IS coming. Now come on, let's go to the Labor Day parade together."

Now Halloween is a really fun day! On October 31, this day is celebrated as a special holiday for children to dress up in all kinds of funny costumes to go begging for treats when it gets dark outside. The children knock on their neighbor's doors and say in a very loud voice, "TRICK OR TREAT!" Moms make costumes for their children on their sewing machines or purchase them from department or toy stores. Some children dress up in their mom's or dad's shoes (that are too big for them) and their hats and long clothes (these are too big, too). The girls put their mom's red lipstick on their lips and use their eyebrow pencils to make beauty moles on their cheeks. Boys paint masks on their faces, using red and black washable paint. Then they spend their time scaring the girls with their monster makeup. It's a lot of fun when it's time for classroom parties at school. There is apple bobbing, where the water tickles your nose if you stick you face in the water too deep. There is even a contest for dancing and one to pick the scariest costume. Everybody is excited about Halloween—everybody except Bebi.

But she couldn't find her Santa hat, so she doesn't dress up in a costume. She doesn't want to go "trick or treating" when it gets dark. All she can think of are the treats she gets on Christmas day. She walks over to her teacher, Mrs. Rayford, with the picture of Santa she made and gloomily asks, "But, when is **Christmas** coming?" Mrs. Rayford tells her, "Christmas is coming soon Bebi. Try to enjoy Halloween today."

19

The last Thursday in November is Thanksgiving Day. To celebrate this holiday, people look forward to sharing big dinners with family and friends to show how happy they are for all the good things they have. Dad goes to the turkey farm and brings home the biggest turkey he can find! It is so heavy, he has to carry it on his shoulder! Mom roasts the turkey in the oven until it's golden brown. Then she makes corn bread dressing to stuff inside the turkey. When it's time to sit down and eat dinner, Dad carves the turkey while Mom slices many cinnamon-flavored, buttery-tasting pieces of sweet potato pie for dessert. You can't get a taste of pie unless you eat all of your food. So everybody is ready to eat everything on their plate—except Bebi.

She doesn't want any turkey with dressing. She doesn't want any sweet potato pie either. Bebi only wants to know, "But, when is **Christmas** coming?" Dad says to her, "Christmas is coming real soon now Bebi. You just wait and see." Little Bebi doesn't believe that Christmas is coming real soon though. Everybody has been telling her to wait and wait. They have told her, "Christmas is coming soon," and Bebi has wondered to herself, "When is soon? Is tomorrow soon?" Still there has been no Christmas—yet!

It seems everybody knows that Christmas is coming soon because the Friday after Thanksgiving Day is the busiest shopping day in the whole year! People are eager to start buying the gifts they will give to one another on Christmas Day. They wake up early to get to the stores as soon as they open. Mom and Auntie Kathy go to the mall where they shop for gifts all day. Cousin Kara comes to stay with Bebi and her sisters. Dad, Uncle Gus and Cortez go to the woods to chop down a tall pine Christmas tree. The tree they find always seems to be the biggest and greenest Dad has ever picked! It seems almost as tall as the house! The leaves on it are so thick you can't even see the tree trunk. The tree stands in the front window of the living room, so at night, when the lights are turned on, you can see what a beautiful tree it is from outside the window. When they get home with the tree, the smell of pine fills every room in the house. Dad takes all the Christmas tree decorations down from the attic. Everybody is excited and helps to put the decorations on the tree! There are different-colored, Italian-styled lights—some blink on and off—green and red tinsel—long, thin, silver strips of paper foil—green garlands and little snowmen with black stovetop hats. There are decorations that have been collected by Mom and Dad over 10 years! For the very top of the tree, a silver angel with gold-glittered wings is carefully unwrapped. Dad himself places the angel on top of the tree after all the other decorations are on.

Bebi doesn't want to go shopping. She doesn't want to help put the decorations on the tree. She doesn't care about Dad, Uncle Gus and Cortez going to the woods to chop down a tree. Bebi only wants to know, "But, when is **Christmas** coming?" When Auntie Kathy sees that Bebi isn't helping with the decorating, she tells her, "Christmas is coming really soon now. Be a good girl and help us get ready for Christmas."

Many more days go by and more shopping is done. All the presents that have been bought by everybody are wrapped and placed under the huge tree. Bebi doesn't want to wrap any presents. She doesn't want to shop for gifts. She just wants to know, "When is **Christmas** coming?"

Then early on December 25 while everybody in the DeLoach family's house is still sleeping—everybody except Bebi—Bebi hears a noise and comes downstairs to see if Mom is in the kitchen cooking breakfast.

When she gets to the kitchen, she doesn't see Mom, so she calls out, "Mommy, where are you?"

When her mom doesn't answer, Bebi tiptoes quietly into the living room to see if that is where she heard the noise.

When she looks into the living room, Bebi's eyes grow wide! To her delight she sees all kinds of toys and gifts under the huge tree! There is the red bicycle with a red and white straw basket she really, really wanted! She is sure the rag doll with stringy, yarn hair is hers! The guitar and the drums that lay near the tree just has to be from Santa. There is even a green spinning top with a wooden handle! A toy baking oven with a very tiny box of cake mix is under the tree. She sees toy dishes sitting on top of a little table and chair set! There is a camera, a watch, some new red, shiny boots, a radio with earphones and a baby doll as tall as Bebi!

Outside the snow is falling in soft clumps. Bebi knows this is the special kind of snow she and her brother use to make a fat snowman after all the gifts are opened. All the tree branches are glistening and bending under the weight of the snow! The ground is covered with a thick blanket of white, fluffy snow! The Christmas tree lights on all the neighbor's houses are still lit, and boy, are they sparkling and pretty! The sun even seems to be shining extra bright! When she looks around the room, Bebi notices that the glass of milk Mommy left on the table near the fireplace is now half-gone and the cookie that was left right by it has a big bite out of it! There's Christmas candy, apples, bananas, oranges and different kinds of nuts in a big, round, gold-colored fruit basket on the living room table! Bebi knew that finally, Christmas WAS here! She ran as fast as her little legs could run, back through the kitchen and up the stairs!

First she went to Mom and Dad's bedroom! She jumped on their bed and shouted, "Wake up Mommy! Daddy, wake up!

CHRISTMAS IS HERE!"

T hen she ran into Zindzi's room and jumped on her bed.
She bounced up and down, then up and down again,
all the while shouting, "Wake up Zindzi! Wake up!

CHRISTMAS
IS
HERE!"

Bebi didn't stop shouting until she woke everybody in
the house! She led them all, marching behind her
in a line, down the stairs, then through
the kitchen and into
the living room.

Pointing to the toys under the tree, she said in her very loud squeaky voice, "See, I told you Christmas was coming! **And look—**"

"CHRISTMAS IS HERE!"